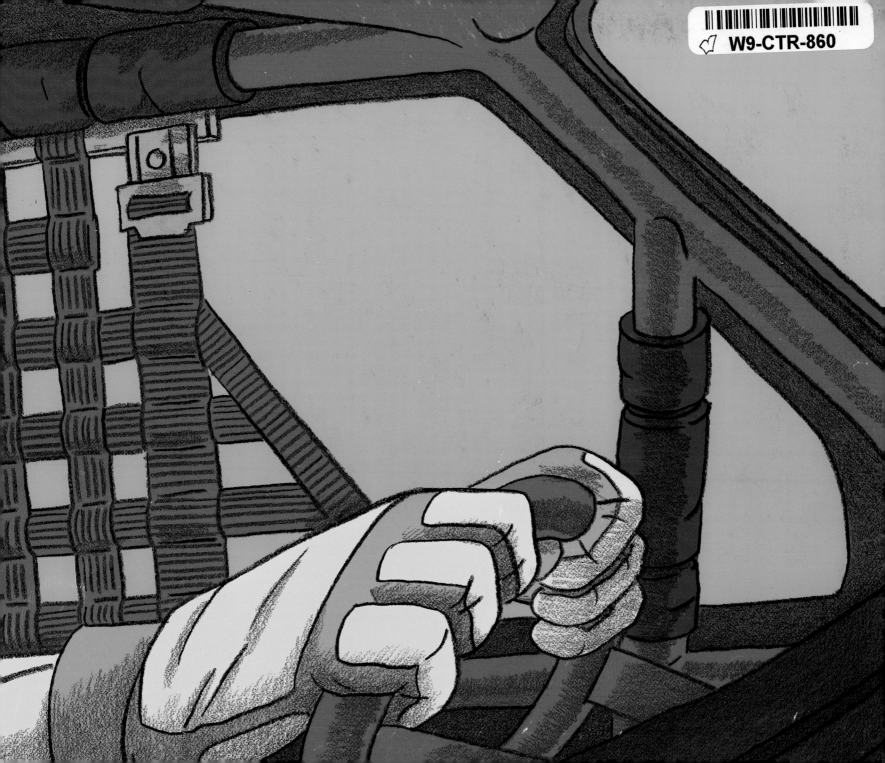

Henry Holt and Company, LLC, *Publishers since 1866*, 175 Fifth Avenue, New York, New York 10010
www.henryholtchildrensbooks.com

Henry Holt® is a registered trademark of Henry Holt and Company, LLC.

Library of Congress Cataloging-in-Publication Data
Rex, Michael. My race car / Michael Rex.
Summary: A simple presentation of a race car and how it is used and serviced during a race.
1. Automobiles, Racing—Juvenile literature. 2. Automobile racing—Juvenile literature.
[1. Automobiles, Racing. 2. Automobile racing.] I. Title.
TL236.R47 2000 629.228—dc21   99-31773
The illustrations in this book were done in pencil; color was added using Adobe® Graphic Software.

ISBN-13: 978-0-8050-6101-7 / ISBN-10: 0-8050-6101-0
First Edition—2000 / Manufactured in China on acid-free paper. ∞
3 5 7 9 10 8 6 4

My Race Car

Michael Rex

Henry Holt and Company ⬤ New York

To Steve, for the house calls

I have a race car. I drive it all the time.

Today is the big race.
My crew and I are getting ready.
We work on the engine so that
it runs perfectly.
Without a good crew,
I have no chance of winning.

My Crew!

When I race I wear a flame resistant suit and boots. My suit is yellow and green, and it matches my car.

I fasten my seat belts—one over each shoulder and one across my lap.

I put on my gloves, and strap my helmet on tight.

I drive my car to the starting line. I am ready to race.

Thousands of people watch as we take a few warm-up laps around the

track and wait for the green flag. The green flag means go. **GO!**

My car is a stock car.
It can go 175 miles per hour, and sometimes faster!

My car weighs more than 4,000 pounds.
That's as much as ten gorillas!

I make a pit stop. My crew changes all four tires and

fills up my gas tank. The pit stop takes less than 30 seconds.

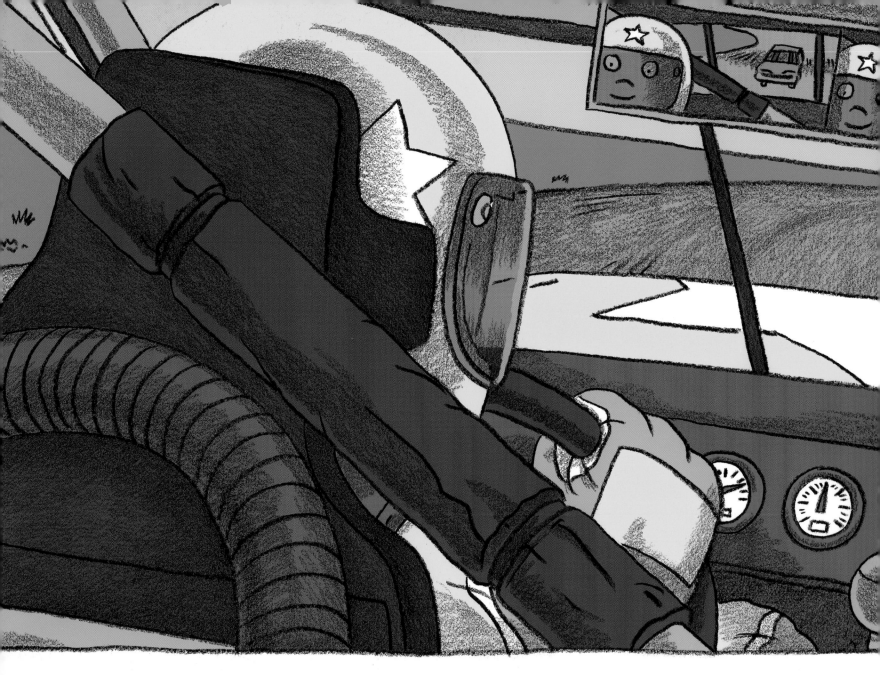

I'm off again driving quickly, but safely.
We race for 500 miles.

That's 250 times around the track!
This takes about three and a half hours.

Uh-oh, the first-place car has lost control. It's spinning out!
The second-place car tries to avoid hitting it, and spins out, too.

I pass the wreck. Both drivers are safe.

The roll cages in their cars saved them.
The roll cage is a big, strong frame
around the driver's seat.

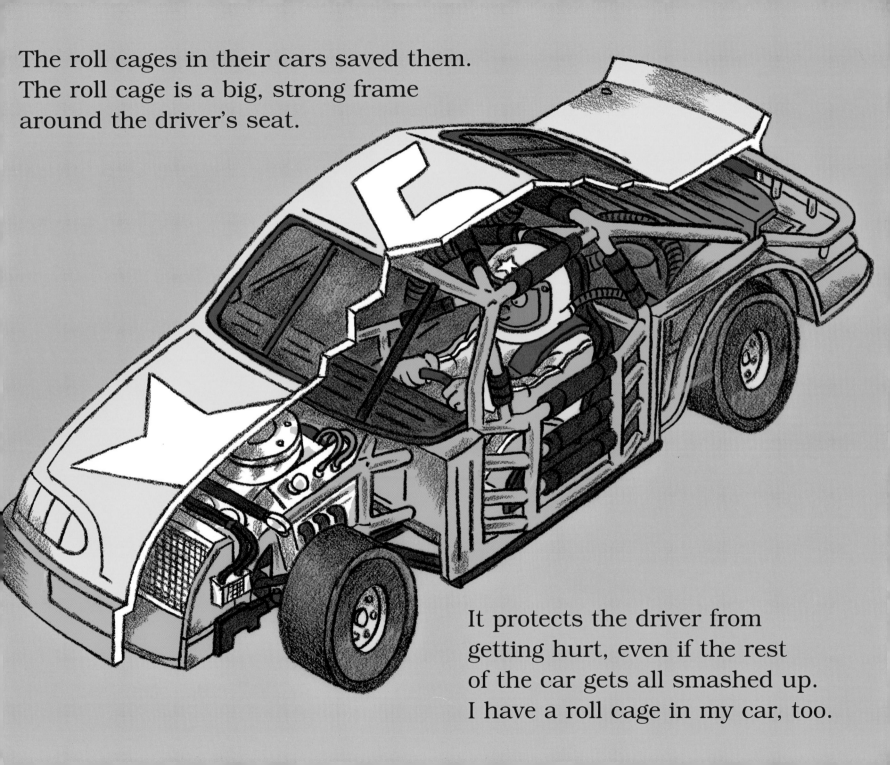

It protects the driver from
getting hurt, even if the rest
of the car gets all smashed up.
I have a roll cage in my car, too.

I am in first place now, ahead of all the other cars, but it's a close race.

The checkered flag is waving! I win the race!

The crew and I receive
a trophy . . .

. . . and for my special prize, a ceremonial first-place milk shake!